# New Home, New Friends

SRA

Columbus, OH

# SRAonline.com

Send all inquiries to this address:
SRA/McGraw-Hill
4400 Easton Commons
Columbus, OH  43219

ISBN: 978-0-07-608772-3
MHID: 0-07-608772-7

2 3 4 5 6 7 8 9  NOR  13  12  11  10  09

The camp did not look like much to Charlie. He and his papa and his younger brother had spent months traveling from New York to California. *It isn't really a town at all,* he thought. The signs of prosperity he had expected from a gold mining camp were nowhere to be seen. Dust and dirt were everywhere. *The buildings aren't even really buildings,* he thought. Buildings back home were well constructed and sturdy. He looked at the patched lean-tos resting against one another.

Shabby white and not-so-white tents stood in rows, and one tent was even made of branches and tattered shirts. Only one real building was visible in the whole town. The sign on the front read "Sam's General Store." Charlie tapped his brother Jackson on the shoulder. "We need to buy supplies," he said.

They walked toward the general store, careful to avoid a mud-filled trench in the street. Jackson was almost exploding with excitement. "We're here, Charlie, in a real, live mining camp!"

Charlie was not sure why his brother was so excited. Were they looking at the same thing? He had not seen any other children since they had arrived in Columbia, California.

They had left all their friends and most of their belongings in New York City. There had been room for only necessities on the journey to California. But Charlie missed his mother most of all. She had stayed behind. Papa would send for her after he had staked his claim, and then they would all be together again.

Charlie reminded Jackson, "After we buy supplies, we need to set up the tent."

Their papa had left for the gold fields as soon as they had reached the mining camp that morning. Charlie knew that Papa would not be back until nightfall and he would be tired and hungry. It was up to Charlie to find food and water for the night. He was the oldest at sixteen—practically a man.

Charlie strode into the general store with Jackson at his heels. The store had a dirt floor, barrels and shelves in every available nook and cranny, and prices that made Charlie gasp. His papa had not given him enough money to buy much, at least not at these prices.

"May I have five pounds of flour and a pound of butter?" Charlie said. That was all they could afford, though he longed for a taste of taffy. He decided not to think about that.

Charlie paid the man behind the counter and asked, "How's the hunting around here?"

"The hunting in this territory is the best around!" the man replied. "The woods are crawling with critters—squirrels, rabbits, you name it."

Charlie and Jackson loaded up their supplies and headed for the rows of tents. They needed to find a place to pitch their tent for the night. Then Charlie would have to go into the woods and hunt for food.

"Jackson, you're going to have to wait here and guard our belongings," he said. "Maybe I can snare a rabbit or something."

"I want to go with you!" Jackson objected. "I want to see what's out there."

Jackson was only twelve and would be safer at the camp. "You need to stay here," Charlie said. "I should be back in a couple of hours. The man said it wasn't far."

Jackson was not happy, but he obeyed his brother.

After Charlie had gone, Jackson decided to unpack the cooking supplies from the wagon. When Papa got back, he would want everything ready so he could cook dinner.

After he had finished, Jackson was bored and wanted to talk to Charlie. He looked at the sun's position to gauge how much time had passed, but he was sure it had been more than two hours since his brother had left.

He looked in the direction Charlie had headed. There was still no sign of him. It seemed as though centuries had passed.

Jackson knew they would need firewood to cook dinner. He also was concerned about his big brother. So he left a note for his father pinned to the wagon and strode off toward the forest.

Jackson had lived in the city his whole life. Even after the long journey west, the forest still frightened him. He took a deep breath and walked into the woods. Jackson nervously fingered the marbles in his pocket. They reminded him of happy mornings spent playing with friends back east. He started to relax and began gathering wood.

Charlie was fine, Jackson told himself. He was as big and strong as a bear! Jackson bent down to grab a fallen branch and when he looked up, four young Paiutes were standing in front of him.

They had appeared out of nowhere. Jackson opened his mouth to yell for help, but then he realized something. They were children, just like him, and they looked as scared as he did.

There were three girls. One was about his age, and another looked a little older. A little boy stood behind the oldest girl, clutching her leg. Jackson thought they must be related from the protective way they stood over the youngest.

The oldest one seemed to make a decision. "Charlie?" she said and then waited to see if Jackson recognized the word.

"Charlie!" he replied, nodding vigorously. Did they know where his brother was?

The girl took him by the hand and tugged. "Charlie," she said firmly.

As they walked Jackson held out his hand to the little boy. He said, "My name is Jackson."

The little boy giggled and took his hand. "Jackson?" he whispered.

They walked together until they came to a clearing, and Jackson spotted Charlie leaning against a tree. His leg was propped up, and he had a sheepish expression on his face.

Charlie said, "I don't know what I would have done if they hadn't found me. I twisted my ankle pretty good."

Jackson helped his brother to his feet and chose a stick from the wood he had bundled up for firewood. "You can use this stick as a cane, Charlie," he said.

"It's perfect, Jackson," Charlie replied. He turned to the others and said, "Thank you."

"Yes, thank you for helping my brother," Jackson said. He thought about his marbles and his friends back home. Then he stepped forward and placed one of his best marbles into the little boy's palm. "Friends!" Jackson said.

"Friends?" the boy repeated, whispering. "Friends!"

# Vocabulary

**prosperity** (pros per´ i tē) (page 3) *n.* Success, wealth, or good fortune.

**tattered** (tat´ ərd) (page 4) *adj.* Torn into shreds.

**trench** (trench) (page 4) *n.* A long narrow ditch.

**longed** (longd) (page 7) *v.* Past tense of **long:** To want very much; yearn.

**territory** (ter´ i tôr´ ē) (page 8) *n.* A large area or region of land.

**centuries** (sen´ chə rēz) (page 10) *n.* Plural of **century:** A period of one hundred years.

**bundled** (bun´ dəld) (page 15) *v.* Past tense of **bundle:** To tie or wrap together.

# Comprehension Focus: Predicting

1. Reread page 10. What did you predict had happened to Charlie?

2. Do you predict that Charlie and Jackson will develop a friendship with the Paiute children? Why or why not?